I0738936

Church Ladies' Coffee

Robin Wettergren Bauer

Preface: This is a story about several families who have been devastated by their loved ones being in the wrong place at the wrong time. The occurrences were preventable. The culprit: error in judgment and decision-making. This could easily happen to any of us. All it takes is a split second of confusion, or eyes and mind not being focused. All families involved were wishing there was a way to turn back the clock. Forgiveness is never verbally mentioned, nor expected. The story takes an unusual path when they selflessly come together to help a friend in need, and Ed Wright, from the *Stone Creek Herald* is there to capture this amazing story. Grief and emotional pain take a detour. The victims do their best to put aside their anguish, so they can focus on helping their friend.

Location: Stone Creek, Minnesota, a river city nestled along the Minnesota River, approximately thirty-four miles southwest of Minneapolis. Population 13,290.

Messages: This book delivers a potpourri of messages, with the hope that the reader keeps them in the back of their mind, as they go about their daily living.

Dedication: This book is dedicated to volunteers, whether serving in an organization, or lending a helping hand to a neighbor or stranger in need. Where would the world be without volunteers? This book is also dedicated to my husband, Dave. He has made our almost thirty-seven years of marriage far from dull, and is my champion, who is there to say "good for you, dear."

Disclaimer: This is a work of fiction. Names, characters, businesses, places, events, and incidents are either the products of the author's imagination or used in a fictitious manner, with the exception of a few historical events.

Disclaimer on the disclaimer: The author does have a soft spot for chardonnay and mozzarella sticks. And, her husband really did make over a dozen copies of the "you're still wrong" note and planted them throughout the house.

The story takes place between April 2016 and May 2017.

Prologue

April 2016

Natalie Carter was finally starting to come out of her shell. Losing her husband, Tanner, suddenly and out of the blue didn't register at times. Although a year had passed, she still finds herself waiting for him to walk through the door. After twenty-seven years of marriage, it was taking awhile to get used to the empty stool at the kitchen island. An unsolicited "life is for the living" message is what she'd often hear, and tried to keep in mind. She thought it helped to keep the same routine, which was to start out mornings with a walk, then coffee and a treat at Church Ladies' Coffee (CLC). She found familiar faces and brief conversations with the owner comforting.

CLC served egg coffee, the same as one would find served at a church when there was a rummage sale, a church dignitary, and, of course, funerals. Egg coffee is time-consuming to make, but rich in flavor. CLC was the only coffee shop in town that served it. No other coffee shop wanted the mess it entailed: bringing water to a rapid boil in an enamel pot, adding a mixture of eggs with coffee grounds, then adding cold water to settle the grounds. The menu board on the wall referred to it as the CLC special. "Hit me with a CLC special," customers would say.

Elsie Swanson was the owner and manager of the most visited coffee shop in town. She was sixty-four with platinum hair and hazel brown eyes. According to a newly revised BMI (body/mass/index) chart, she was twenty-seven pounds overweight. She was not sold on these new standards and questioned the BMI formula her clinic used, and, as far as she was concerned, her business depended on the taste of her goods. Hence, a few pounds of extra weight didn't hurt.

She was comfortable with her body shape, and it showed. Self-confidence was one of her attributes. She also had an eye for repurposing furniture and such. Her favorite television channel was HGTV, and her favorite website was Pinterest.

She discovered the city of Stone Creek back in 2003, while passing through on her way to Chanhassen, Minnesota. She and some friends had tickets to the Chanhassen Dinner Theater. Their van started to act up, so they pulled over a block off Stone Creek's main drag.

She instantly noticed an abandoned building along the river. It happened to be an old dairy with a *FOR SALE* sign. Another of Elsie's traits was vision. She was drawn to the building like iron to a magnet. Two months later she was the owner. Even though she knew nothing about running a business, she was a quick learner and had guidance from the Small Business Association.

The atmosphere of CLC was warm and inviting. Elsie had collected some interesting pieces throughout the years, which added to the shop's charm. For many customers, CLC felt like a home away from home. There was a designated area for card players, mostly seniors, as well as a little nook for young children, and, eventually, a hangout room for anyone else who cared to hang out. Elsie picked up books and puzzles at garage sales, but she mostly relied on Nat, aka the Yard Sale Junkie, to be on the lookout for certain pieces—mainly lamps, pictures, furniture, and occasional odds and ends.

Like Nat, Elsie had a fondness for castaway things—things that others might feel were too far gone to be saved or redeemed or repurposed. Heck, she'd found that most of these things just needed a new home; a second chance to be useful. She didn't mind imperfections—the occasional bend in a pie tin or scratch on a frame.

Elsie brewed coffee and baked sweets, and saw her life as one of service. She was no stranger to the pain of losing a loved one. Her beloved nephew was killed in a college campus shooting. It was the same old story that appeared over and over again in the news. She practically raised her nephew, and was proud of how he turned out. Her brother and sister-in-law spent too much time down at the local watering hole, neglecting him. She was reminded by her friends and loved ones that life is for the living, and getting back into her work was the best thing for her. She found herself sharing that statement with others, however, at times it was easier said than done. She wished she could turn back time.

Kelly Henderson, a junior at the local high school, wished too she could turn back time. Hers was a day in April of 2015, when, due to spring flooding, she took a different, unfamiliar route home from school. She, with cell phone in hand, had responded to a text. One letter, a quick "K," and she'd blown through a stop sign.

And, since the year before, another resident also wished for the miracle to turn back time. Harlan Hansen was too proud to give up the keys to his car and because of this, time stopped in August of 2014 for seven-year-old Matthew McAnders, son of Jake and Lisa McAnders, who'd been pulling his red wagon in front of his house. Not a day passes that Harlan doesn't hear the thud of Matthew against the car.

No matter what side of the heartbreak, every tragedy has its own course, and its own map. Eventually the paths of Nat, Kelly, Harlan, and Jake intersect, and it happened at Church Ladies' Coffee. Although there were no words spoken of forgiveness, and none expected, each eventually made the decision to move on. "Life is for the living."

One

She did it again. Natalie Carter, called Nat by her friends, had one too many mozzarella sticks. She felt full, tired, and all talked out. Per usual, chardonnay fueled her desire for fried cheese. Nat was convinced they were the perfect pairing.

All the same, it was time to head home, and she bid farewell to her former co-workers, whom she met for happy hour. She hadn't seen them since the memorial service for her late husband, Tanner. A drink with friends was a baby step to getting out and about. It sort of felt good. She had limited herself to a glass of wine, and nursed it slowly, so it would last two hours, giving her time to catch up on office scuttlebutt.

Her former co-workers had made several attempts to get together, but it was only recently that Nat felt like socializing. She had finally listened to what seemed like wise words from Elsie, the owner of Church Ladies' Coffee, the local coffee and pastry shop Nat frequented. Elsie would remind Nat that life was for the living, and that Nat owed it to her family to live.

As Nat drove home she realized a year had passed since the memorial service. Last April provided some unusually warm days compared to this April. Had it not been a warm April day, Tanner wouldn't have been test-driving a motorcycle. Nat was a block from home when she noticed a warning light appeared on the dashboard of her SUV. It was too late to pull into Londer's Chevrolet so she added the task to her list of errands for the next day. Londer's is where Tanner took their vehicles. Nat trusted Willy, a long-term service technician, to fix any problem without unnecessary repairs.

Nat was beat. She sifted through the mail, most of it junk, and then off to bed she went. Putting her legs up felt good. She started to take on a habit of Tanner's that she hadn't cared for while he was alive—and that was flipping through a dozen or so channels using the remote, and then falling asleep with the remote in hand.

It was 11:15 pm when the cell phone rang and startled her. It was Hazel, her neighbor from across the street. She called to let Nat know the garage door was open. "Thanks, Hazel," said a sleepy Nat. "I owe you one—*again*."

The alarm clock went off at 7:00 am. It seemed as though Nat had just shut the garage door for the night. She hit the snooze a few times before getting up. Her daily ritual required stopping at Church Ladies' Coffee for a white chocolate raspberry scone and coffee.

A few miles away, inside a remodeled, well-maintained brick rambler lived Harlan and Dorothy Hansen. The sound of a television in unison with a radio, with both volume controls being set too high, could be heard outside. The mail carrier always got a chuckle. The television is situated in the den, while the radio is on the kitchen counter.

The landline phone rings.

"Yes, just a minute I can't hear a word you're saying," said Dorothy in a frustrated manner. "Let me turn the radio off." Dorothy scurried across the kitchen while trying to carry on a conversation with Ed Wright, columnist for the *Stone Creek Herald*. The old landline phone was situated on the kitchen counter. It was a princess trimline, pinkish-beige in color, and was *the* kind of phone to have back in the 1970s. Placed under it is a phonebook with scribbled names and numbers of frequently called people. Many of the scribbles have started to fade, and many numbers were crossed out.

"That's right, Ed. Harlan has completed his 100 hours of community service, but I think he will continue to give talks down at the senior center. He feels an obligation, and that his story might prevent an incident similar to his."

The managing editor of *Stone Creek Herald* assigned Ed Wright to do a story featuring community service as it related to hours sentenced by a judge. Harlan Hansen was Ed's main focus—at this point. The managing editor knew Ed had the right connections which would lead to a story that delivered a message.

Harlan's "being fit to drive" talks had struck a chord. Ed was experiencing somewhat of the same situation. Not with his elderly parents, as one might have assumed, but with his twin sister, who was in poor health and on several medications. His parents, who were in their early eighties, were still sharp-minded and their reflexes were amazing for their age. They walked around the indoor community track almost every day.

"The past two years have been tough," Dorothy shared with Ed, as she had done so many times before. "Our lives haven't been the same and never will be. If only we had listened to our children. Harlan was stubborn, and worried about how we would get around. Harlan was our designated driver, so I didn't push the idea of his parking his keys for good. We felt like we would have been imposing upon others with asking for rides to church, doctor appointments—you name it. If only that letter from the Department of Motor Vehicles had come a week earlier. It boils down to Harlan being too proud to turn in his keys, and my being concerned about losing our freedom. Do you want to talk to Harlan?"

"Yes," said Ed, "if I didn't catch him at a bad time."

Dorothy noticed her husband of sixty years was fast asleep in his beat-up vinyl recliner.

"Sorry, Ed, I'll have to have him call you later. Looks like he's in a deep sleep. I hate to wake him. Sound sleep is rare since ... the accident."

"That's okay, Dorothy. There's no rush. Have a good day. Bye now."

The judge handed down one hundred hours of community service. Harlan's children helped him create a presentation. His audiences were seniors attending a defensive driving course in order to get a discount on their auto insurance. What he offered was powerful and consisted of his admitting his error in judgment and his stubbornness, which took the life of Matthew McAnders. His talk included a slideshow of signs when it was time someone should give up his or her car keys, and provided several ways on how to cope with losing, what he called "partial" independence. There was no preaching, and he made it clear there was no set age to give up the keys. "No set age" is what some of the audience wanted to hear.

Ed had attended several of Harlan's presentations, mainly to see the reaction from the audience. He still didn't know how he'd write a story. He didn't feel like he had enough. Something was missing. He decided to put the story on the backburner with hopes that eventually something would come along to inspire him. He needed more than statistics. The accident had not only taken its toll on Harlan, but on Dorothy as well. He knew that he needed to proceed with caution as not to drive Harlan into a tunnel of anxiety.

Harlan no longer had a license to drive. He was eighty-nine and his reflexes were not what they used to be. His family physician was not known to have contacted the DMV, even when slowed reflexes were obvious.

Not a day passed that Harlan didn't wish he could roll back time. Roll back the time to 3:47 pm on Friday, August 8, 2014.

He would get a knot in his stomach, whenever he saw a clock with the time of 3:48, as that was the time when his car jumped the curb and struck his neighbor boy, Matthew McAnders. Harlan mistakenly stepped on the gas pedal instead of the brake when backing out of his driveway. If only he would have listened to his children, when they asked him to give up driving. He should have, and he knew it. It would have prevented this nightmare. Deep down he knew the only reason he didn't give up driving was because it made him feel weak. He felt insulted when it came up in a conversation several years ago. Harlan missed helping Matthew with fixing his bike, and just plain having Matthew following him around and asking how things worked.

Two

Nat took a forty-minute walk around the neighborhood and then hopped in the shower. "Crap," she said with a dragged out sigh, as she noticed a lot of steam after exiting the shower. She had forgotten to turn on the fan and open the bathroom door. Her shower had been longer than usual—it was one of those days when she didn't want to get out. "Making the bathroom walls sweat is not what I had in mind," she said to herself. Shortly after Tanner's passing Nat started to talk to herself. She used to think people who talked to themselves were odd.

Within the hour Nat was at the Church Ladies' Coffee, the only coffee shop in town, where the coffee didn't taste like charred sludge with a ridiculous price. The coffee shop was a converted dairy. The outside was painted gray, had black and gray striped awnings, a trellis with blue morning glories, and the famous sign above the entrance, which attracted birds, since there was just enough space in the sign for a bird to build a nest. In the spring there would be countless bird droppings on the sidewalk, not to mention close calls nearly hitting customers. The inside was warm and inviting with dark hickory hardwood flooring, light gray walls, and white enameled trim. The main area, as well as enclaves, were accented with big area rugs, couches, and an eclectic collection of tables and chairs. Something for everyone's taste. There was also a nice assortment of greeting cards.

"Would you like the usual, Nat?" asked Elsie, the owner. Elsie knew Nat was wild about the egg coffee. Nat didn't like strong coffee, nor cared for cream, sugar, or any of the fancy stuff. She just wanted her coffee plain and simple, yet rich.

"Sounds good," said Nat who seemed to be preoccupied, more than usual. So much so that she didn't bother to look at the charge card, after making her purchase of a CLC special and a white chocolate raspberry scone. Elsie was multi-tasking. She had two charge cards on the counter, both similar in color and logo. Nat always sat and read the complimentary daily paper, while she enjoyed her morning fix. Elsie stocked the coffee shop with the *Stone Creek Herald, Wall Street Journal, Minneapolis Star Tribune,* and *St. Paul Pioneer Press.*

"Jake, hey, Jakester! Jakemeister! Jake-a-rama! Your coffee is going to get cold," announced Elsie in her stern, yet friendly reminder voice. Jake was looking at the greeting cards, shaking his head.

"Jake will do for my name," he said with a smirk. Usually he didn't mind the teasing, but this time it seemed to catch a lot of attention from customers he didn't know. "By the way, why are greeting cards so expensive?" he asked Elsie, while he picked up his coffee and white chocolate raspberry scone.

"I haven't a clue. I only add 20 percent onto the wholesale price, which accounts for time to stock, and miscellaneous inventory tasks. Here's your charge card."

Jake happened to notice the name on the card was not his. It read "Natalie R. Carter." "Uhhh, Elsie, my name isn't Natalie," said Jake. "By any chance do you know a Natalie R. Carter?"

"I'm sooooo sorry," said Elsie with an apologetic voice. "Your two cards were the only ones on the counter, so she must have yours. Natalie is over there at the table in the corner, towards the newspaper rack. Would you mind making the switch?"

"No problem," said Jake looking over at Nat. "Looks like Natalie Carter and I both have good taste in scones. I'll be happy to ask her to switch cards."

Elsie didn't make matchmaking a habit, but she knew both Jake and Natalie well and had a feeling they had a lot in common, besides their losing a loved one. Even if they never got together as lovebirds, perhaps just having someone to talk to and share a meal now and then would be awesome.

"Excuse me," said Jake. "I believe Elsie inadvertently gave your charge card to me and mine to you." Nat slowly put down the newspaper and tried focusing on what this customer was saying. She looked puzzled for a moment and then realized he was holding her charge card.

"Oh, oh, just a minute, while I dig for your card," said an embarrassed Nat. Her purse was big and stuffed with receipts, reminders, old shopping lists, and notes from Tanner. Tanner was known to stick a "you're still wrong" note to her billfold now and then. Many years ago they had a disagreement and both would remind the other that the other was still wrong. "I'm so sorry. Looks like I need to add a note to clean out my purse. Here's your charge card."

"Thanks," said Jake. He took a table not too far from Nat. He then began to focus on his cell phone—concentrating on emails and text messages. It didn't take him but a few minutes to consume his scone and be on his way. He nodded and smiled at Nat as he got up and made his way out the door. Nat couldn't help notice his nice smile and beautiful teeth.

After Nat finished reading the local paper she headed to Londer's Chevrolet. "Hi Willy," said Nat. "Glad you are able to take a look at my SUV. A warning light came on the dashboard last night, and this morning it started to make a light clunking-thunking noise now and then. Mainly when I'm stopped."

"Why don't you have a seat in the waiting area and I'll run a diagnostic on your dream machine," said Willy. "I know how much this piece of art means to you and that it took Tanner years to get you an all-wheel drive." They both laughed, because it was true.

"At least he could see how much I enjoyed it while he was still alive," Nat said with a whisper and a wink. "I told Tanner I'd drive it until it drops."

Nat made herself comfortable in the waiting room, where there were magazines and a television. After thirty minutes Willy came to tell Nat that he had good news and bad news. The good news being that an issue with the exhaust system, which was fairly reasonable to replace, caused the clunking. However, the thunking meant the transmission was going out. Nat agreed to go ahead with the repairs. She said she would wait, even though it would be several hours before it was completed. She had her cell phone and new computer tablet to keep her occupied. Having time to kill would give her an opportunity to learn the ins and outs of the tablet.

She was curious about this Jake person at Church Ladies' Coffee. She knew he was a regular but never paid attention to him. As she handed his credit card back to him earlier that morning, she noticed that his last name was McAnders. The name sounded familiar—she had heard it before. She then did her first search using the tablet. She typed in Jake McAnders of Stone Creek, Minnesota. An obituary appeared showing the words "survived by Jake and Lisa McAnders." Matthew McAnders was Jake's son. A wave of compassion for the family passed through Nat.

After Nat finished with reading about Jake McAnders, she flipped through the television channels. The presidential election pretty much took over all channels. She was, like most, fed up with such nasty ads. She thought it was amazing how low some of the candidates could stoop. Just as Willy poked his head through the waiting room door to tell Nat the work was completed, they both noticed the words BREAKING NEWS on the television. It was reported that there had been a death at Paisley Park, Prince's studio, located a few miles down the road, and updates would be provided as more information became available. "What a shocker," said Nat as she tucked the computer tablet inside her purse.

"It sure is," Willy said handing her the work papers for her signature. "My guess is that Highway 5 is going to get pretty congested." To Nat's surprise the traffic flow wasn't an issue. Her route home took her past Paisley Park. She could have taken a back-way home, but she like others was curious. The Carver County Sheriff's Department seemed to already have things under control.

Three

The next day Nat's daughters stopped over. It was an unannounced visit. The three of them sat around the kitchen island, which was always the spot for hanging out, as well as sharing meals. The dining room table was rarely used. Nat was glad she and Tanner had moved to a townhome. It ended up being a godsend for Nat, as the mowing, raking, and snow removal was handled by the homeowners association. The 2500-square-foot townhome made it easy to maintain. There were lots of windows, which provided ample sunlight. Of all the rooms in the townhome, Nat's favorite room had been the pantry where she would sit on a stool and browse through cookbooks. After Tanner's passing, the pantry had become her crying booth. In addition to cookbooks and canned items, would be a box of tissues. A good cry always made her feel better. After a few months the pantry was used less and less as a crying booth.

After a few minutes the purpose of Sarah and Sadie's visit was clear.

"Mom, let us plan a fiftieth birthday party for you," said Sarah, Nat's oldest daughter.

"We can make it real simple, just appetizers, cake, and beverages. Please," pleaded Sadie, Nat's youngest daughter. "You really need to start socializing."

Nat reminded both daughters that she doesn't mind being alone. She was used to it when their father traveled. She kept busy with providing townies with rides to their medical appointments, and had a few photography jobs lined up. Also keeping her busy was the task of going through Tanner's belongings. The tough part was to figure out what to do with Tanner's guns. He won one too many over the years at Duck's Unlimited banquets.

"Girls, perhaps you can help research on the best way to sell guns," said Nat. "I don't want them getting into the wrong hands."

"You're changing the subject, Mom," said Sadie.

"Back to your party," said Sarah.

Nat deliberately changed the subject again. "Oh, by the way, I'm taking an online Understanding Investments 101 course," she proudly reported. "Kind of like those intro courses for dummies." She knew who to contact and how to access the online financial portfolios, but now she was accountable for doing the occasional spot-checking, and learning how to make heads or tails out of them. While Tanner was alive he had encouraged Nat to participate in the portfolio reviews, but she procrastinated.

"Back to your party!" said Sarah.

"We're not leaving until we have something fun with friends and family lined up," said Sadie as she searched the Internet for venues. "Your changing the subject is only dragging it out."

"It's only late April and my birthday isn't until September, why the rush to plan now?" asked Nat. Sarah reminded her mother that schedules fill up fast and they wanted to get a SAVE THE DATE card mailed in the next few months, hence firming up details such as location, food, entertainment, and guests.

"Okay, okay," Nat said reluctantly. "Just something short and sweet—and not at my place. I don't want to have to worry about cleaning things like the top of the fridge."

"I got it!" said Sadie excitedly, like she had just won a prize on a TV game show. "We can use the party room at my apartment. It's really nice, and it only requires a damage deposit. We can bring in our own food and beverages—including your chardonnay, mom. A friend of mine had a party there last week. There's a kitchen, and lots of room."

"Okay, okay, but again, let's keep this shindig small—and set a time limit of three hours," said Nat. "While you're here, can you take a look at my laptop? I keep on getting a pop-up message. Sure hope there isn't a virus or some kind of hacking. Computers are great when they work, but not fun when they don't.

"Give me a minute," said Sarah while she made her way to the guest bathroom. "I drank too much iced tea."

As Sarah made her way back to the kitchen island, she noticed that her father's eyeglasses were still on the accent table in the hallway, covered by a clear glass bowl. Tanner had left his good pair of glasses on the table before he left for the motorcycle dealership. He always wore his old pair of sunglasses when riding. Nat couldn't bring herself to put the glasses away, so she placed a clear glass bowl upside down over his glasses and dusted around the bowl.

"Mom, don't you think it's about time to put Dad's eyeglasses away?" asked Sarah with a combination of concern and sadness in her voice. "If you *have to* keep his glasses out, why not put them in a shadow box or display case? I think Dad would agree with me."

While Sarah was inquiring about the glasses, Sadie had figured out the issue with the laptop. It needed an update of some sort.

"Mom," said Sadie as she closed the laptop. "A reminder not to open emails if you don't recognize the sender's name, and don't click on those advertisements and fake news."

"Yes, dear. I appreciate the reminder. I had all that training at work, except the clicking on ads. Too bad those hackers and other computer geniuses can't put their skills to good use. I'm even afraid to place online orders, but it's so convenient."

The girls left feeling like they had made a major breakthrough in getting their mother to agree on having a fiftieth birthday party.

Nat's birthday wasn't until September 17th so the girls had plenty of time to plan and organize. Before Sarah and Sadie left they asked their mother for a guest list. They knew Elsie and some of the usuals at the coffee shop would be on the list for sure.

It was the last Saturday in April, and the April showers had been far and few between. On this particular Saturday, there wasn't a cloud in the sky, yet Nat had entered CLC with an umbrella. Elsie noticed Nat closing the umbrella. Elsie with her head half-cocked yelled across the room and asked about the need for an umbrella when there wasn't any rain in the forecast. Nat didn't want the other customers to hear the explanation, so she walked over to Elsie and explained the close calls with the robin's droppings. Nat suggested that offering regular customers an umbrella with a CLC logo might be a good way to advertise. Elsie half-joking said she'd consider it.

One of the customers blurted out what they had just read on their cell phone. There had been another shooting at a college campus. All chatter stopped for a few minutes as customers checked their cell phones.

Elsie shook her head in dismay. She felt a pit in her stomach, as it brought back memories of her nephew being shot several years ago while teaching at a college in Illinois. An unstable student open fired on students and teachers.

"When will it stop?" she said with tears in her eyes. "Things have gotten worse, not better." Nat could tell that the loss of Elsie's nephew left a deep hole in her heart.

Four

Nat pulled up to CLC shortly before 8:00 am. It was the third Friday in May. There weren't too many vehicles in the parking lot. The blue morning glories on the trellis were gorgeous. One could tell that the shrubs and flowers had just been given a drink. Everything seemed fresh, including the sixty-degree air. Nat walked in and received a natural high from the aroma of coffee and baked goods.

"Top of the morning, Nat," said Elsie. "If you have time I'd like to run something past you after we get you fixed with your coffee and scone."

"Sure," said Nat. In all the years Nat frequented the shop, there were very few times when Elsie had a serious tone in her voice.

"Sid!" shouted Elsie, as she motioned him to cover the front counter. "I'd like you to take over for a few minutes." Sid was a very handsome sixteen year-old African American, who just started at the shop a few weeks ago. At first he was nervous about making change, but after a week it started to come naturally. He preferred dealing with charge cards. Sid was dedicated and conscientious.

Within a few minutes Nat had her order, and she and Elsie were sitting at Nat's usual table. "What's on your mind, Elsie?" asked Nat.

"Well," said Elsie with a deep sigh. "I have somewhat of an uncomfortable situation, and will cut right to the chase. You probably never realized this but Kelly Henderson and her mother have been regular customers for years. Their visits to my shop just happen to be in the afternoon, while your visits are early morning. Kelly saw my help wanted sign and applied. If I hire her she would be here most mornings during the summer, the same time you are here. With the accident and all, her parents have had to dig into their retirement account. They said that she would need to find a way to help pay for college."

"I see your predicament, Elsie," said Nat as her eyes filled up with tears as she had a brief flashback of that horrible day. "I appreciate your taking the time to share this with me."

"Nat, I heard that Kelly is having a hard time—panic attacks and all. Her major is hotel and restaurant management. She thought she'd start small by working in my shop."

"I'm sorry to hear that Kelly and her family are having difficulties. If you think Kelly is qualified for the job, then, by all means … I'll be fine. This will be a good test for me."

As Nat and Elsie were finishing up their conversation, Jake McAnders walked through the door. He was wearing khaki pants, a crisp white tailored shirt, and a raspberry colored tie. The silver streaks in his sandy brown hair complemented his skin tone. Nat guessed he was in his late forties. He always seemed to be in a good mood. Nat was amazed how a person could crack a smile after having gone through such an ordeal. *He must have had one darned good therapist*, she thought.

"Elsie, one of these days a bird is going to poop on one of your customers," said Jake. "By gosh, I hope it's not on me."

"Point well taken, Jake," said Elsie in a frustrated tone. "I'm trying to figure out what to do with that bird and her nest. I don't have the heart to knock down the nest. Yet I have a funny feeling that the bird droppings along the sidewalk might ruin the appetites of a customer or two."

Elsie turned her attention back to Nat, trying to get a sense of how she digested the news. As she got up from the table to make her way back to the front counter, she patted Nat's hand, and the expression on her face signaled appreciation for Nat's understanding when it came to hiring Kelly.

"Thanks for covering the front counter, Sid," said Elsie. "You can go back to keeping your eye on the coffee. The grounds should be settling to the bottom soon." Sid treated CLC like it was his own store. He took pride in working there and took initiative to do things. Elsie knew she struck gold when she hired him and wished she could clone him.

Nat finished her coffee and scone, and then remembered she needed to buy a graduation card for her neighbor, who had finished his masters in something she had never heard of. She got up and made her way to the card racks.

"Any plans for the weekend?" Elsie asked Nat.

"I'm heading up to Brainerd tomorrow and will come back early Sunday," Nat replied, as she was pulling out her money for the card. "I'm going to spend tomorrow with my sister, Gwen, and her husband. We'll probably go for a boat ride, and then head into town for dinner and some pull ta —." As Nat was finishing her sentence her coin purse fell out of her hands, and coins fell in every direction. Jake happened to be walking past and helped pick up Nat's wayward change.

"Shit, I mean thanks for helping, Jake?" replied Nat with a question within a sentence. She had turned three shades of red from embarrassment.

"You're welcome. Your name is Nat, right?" replied Jake with a broad smile. "I think we collected all the coins for your piggy bank."

"Guess it's time to make a stop at the coin counter at the bank. You only saw one coin purse—one of several."

Nat finished paying for the card then made her way towards the door. She and Jake both exited the store at the same time, smiling and nodding at each other. For the first time, their eye contact lasted more than a few seconds.

"Have a good weekend," they both said at the same time, and then laughed.

The alarm buzzed at 6:00 am the next morning, and Nat was on the road by 7:00. She decided to stop for coffee halfway up to Brainerd, rather than stopping at CLC. She made it up to her sister Gwen's house around 9:50 am. The house was located eight miles northwest of Brainerd. Gwen's husband, Corbett, was always thoughtful and accommodating. He bent over backwards making sure things were to Nat's liking. He knew how picky Nat was. The three of them went to an estate sale, boat ride, and topped the evening off with a nice dinner at Pirate's Cove.

"Nat," said, Gwen, "we're wondering how things are going. Tanner's passing is difficult to talk about, and we just don't know what to say. We've even read up on what to say but …"

"Gwen, stop. Just knowing that you and Corbett are here for the girls and me is all I need. Death is an uncomfortable subject. There is no written handbook for this kind of situation. If I ever figure it out I'll let you know. At Tanner's memorial reception line, most people said, 'I'm sorry for your loss.' As redundant as it sounds, there really are no words to convey to those who are grieving, especially with an unexpected loss. It's uncomfortable for all. Just say what comes naturally. Those who are grieving are just happy for the support. Now how about that after dinner drink you have been bragging about? I believe you said this place makes the best chocolate martinis?" Gwen and Nat were glad that Corbett had volunteered to be the designated driver.

The three got back to the house at 10:23 pm. After a few recounts of the night and laughs, Nat made her way to the guest bedroom. Gwen had placed a chocolate mint on Nat's pillow. Nat was touched by the gesture. While trying to get inside the bed Nat discovered an obstacle. Gwen and Corbett had short-sheeted the bed.

The morning came all too quickly, and Nat left shortly after coffee and a homemade caramel roll. She knew the weekenders would be on the road in short order, and glad she didn't pick Memorial Day weekend for her road trip. She was relieved to get home in one piece. Although she left early, the drive on Highway 10 to the outskirts of Stone Creek was a white-knuckle experience. Navigating between vehicles hauling boats and campers wasn't in her comfort zone.

Five

On Monday morning the doorbell rang at 7:30 am. Nat jumped up from a deep sleep, and a good dream. *Damn*, she thought. *Of all times to get woken up—just as I was walking a beach in Hawaii with Steve McGarrett of Hawaii Five-0. And he was to come over for dinner to work on some sort of save the dolphins campaign.*

Nat had slept in her sweat pants and tee-shirt so all she had to do was a quick brush of her hair, and attempt to remove the remnants of her eye makeup. She rarely slept that late in the morning. When she looked through the peephole she saw Chuck, who would do odd jobs for residents in the association.

"Chuck, what an unexpected surprise," mumbled Nat realizing she most likely had morning breath. She kept her lips pretty close together as she spoke.

"Nat," said Chuck, "I'm here to return your special plate, all cleaned up, of course. I'm not able to stick around to help with your usual fix'n things. Last night I had a close call while driving, and it scared me shitless. I was behind the wheel after having too many beers, and shouldn't have been. I've appreciated your kindness, and asking me to do odd jobs around your house, but I need to get some help. Hopefully someday I can return with a clear head, and no shakes. One more thing, I've gained about ten pounds from those chocolate sour cream cookies you send home with me. Those cookies are worth every pound. I suppose you wouldn't give out the recipe?"

"I'm fond of ya, Chuck, but my sister and I swore to keep that recipe a secret. Those cookies make for good fundraising. As for the special plate, you keep it. I bought it at a garage sale not knowing its value. Cost me under a buck. According to eBay it's worth over one hundred. I just want you to have it as a symbol of someone who believes in you. But, you sell it if you need to. Please come back and see me when you are ready. I believe in you. I know it's not a matter of if you come back, but when. We'll celebrate with coffee and chocolate sour cream cookies. Sound like a plan?"

"Will do," said Chuck.

He and Nat exchanged hugs and he was on his way to a treatment center located an hour northeast of Stone Creek. She knew little about him except he was honest and decent. He never spoke of having any close relatives. She knew he served in the Vietnam War, and was tested for Agent Orange. He received a clean bill of health—physically, but the emotional scars remained.

Chuck seemed like a lost soul. And so did Nat. Their stories were different, but yet each had taken their toll. Before Tanner's passing, Nat was used to going to places alone—movies, restaurants, and social functions. Tanner traveled for his job, so Nat made it a point to not revolve her schedule around his, but still the constant empty chair at the kitchen island, when it was occasionally filled, was hard to get used to. Nat thought back to the last time she and Tanner had spoken, and cringed at her harping about his leaving the toilet seat up.

The next morning, Nat was looking at Elsie's new stock of greeting cards. As usual if it was a good card, she would laugh out loud. Harlan was on the other side of the rack and heard laughter. There wasn't much space to browse. He was waiting for her to move. She was in front of all the birthday cards, and the selection on his side was anniversary and sympathy cards.

"Excuse me. I'll be sitting over there," Harlan said, as he pointed to the place where a group of seniors would meet to play card games. "I'm looking for a birthday card for my better half and would appreciate it if you'd let me know when you're done browsing through the birthday cards." The Card Club crew consisted of retirees, all men at this point, with decades of combined work experience. The retirees included a structural engineer, a retired architect, a painter, and, of course, Harlan, a flooring expert.

"Actually, I'm done," said Nat. "Please, take my spot. I'm Nat Carter." She extended her hand.

"I'm Harlan Hansen. Pleasure to meet you. By the sound of your laugh Elsie must have added some funny cards to her collection."

They exchanged a few words, and have a good day nod. As Nat made her way up to the counter to pay for some cards the name Harlan Hansen came to mind. She then realized how he was tied to Jake. *How sad*, she thought.

Before Nat left, she hung up a new sign-up sheet for customers who needed a lift to a medical appointment. She didn't charge for gas. She enjoyed doing it. One customer was a man named Carson, a retired architect. During their commute to his appointments she got to know him well, and admired him. He was eighty-eight years old and a widower. He would talk about his deceased wife, as well as his daughter who lived in Michigan. His mind was sharp, but knew, due to his health, he better leave the driving to others. Now and then there was silence while Nat was driving. When she would look over at Carson she could tell he was in a happy place. She assumed he was thinking about good memories of the past and didn't interrupt with small talk. One day out of the blue, he mentioned how his wife was able to keep the marriage lively. She wanted to meet at the top of the Empire State Building in New York City on their fiftieth wedding anniversary.

"Her wild plan was to meet at the top, engage in a long kiss, and then go somewhere and renew our vows," said Carson. "I believe she had just watched the movie *An Affair to Remember*. I didn't bat an eye, and booked our tickets and hotel room. We had an amazing time. She did things like that. She made life exciting. I was fortunate to have such a fun-loving wife." He chuckled, and never went into detail on how she passed. But, she made him promise not to dwell. Before he knew it, he was at his doctor's appointment. Nat would wait in her SUV. She wanted to give him his independence and privacy.

While Nat was waiting for Carson, she reminisced on decades that had gone before. She thought back to when she and Tanner met on a blind date. She had locked the doors in the vehicle while Carson was at his appointment. An hour later there was a hard knock on the window. It was Carson. This time it was Nat who was in her happy place.

"You must have been having a good daydream," he said after Nat had opened the door. She didn't want to explain that it wasn't a daydream—it was real at one time.

Carson was one of Nat's regulars, who appreciated her offer to provide people with a lift to their appointments. He never shared what kind of doctor he was seeing. She gathered his health issue might be somewhat serious given the names of the specialists on the signage at the medical complex.

As she was driving him back to CLC where he'd meet up with the Card Club crew and get a lift home from one of them, Nat spotted an estate sale sign. She asked Carson if he'd mind if they stopped for a few minutes. He embraced the opportunity. He mentioned his wife also enjoyed going to estate sales, and garage sales. He often accompanied her. *A well-rounded woman,* thought Nat. Nat started her usual browsing and spotted a few unique items. Carson's eyes were magnetized to a table of tools. He noticed there was a one-of-a-kind tool used for architectural drawing. When he inquired as to the price, as there was no sticker, one of the ladies said he could have it for two dollars. Carson tried to remain calm, as he knew it had to be worth way more. These days architectural drawings were pretty much digitized. He hadn't seen this kind of tool in over thirty years. He gladly paid the two dollars.

Nat told Carson if he wanted, she'd be glad to have his company when going to estate and garage sales. He told her he'd be thrilled. He was pleased as punch. Carson was on Nat's schedule for the following week. Nat mentioned that she was on the lookout for some good sales, but there was nothing interesting.

During their usual after appointment commute, Carson mentioned one of his favorite creations. He had designed one of the entertainment band shells in a nearby small town. It was late morning, and Nat didn't have anything pressing for the rest of the day. She asked Carson if he'd like to drive past the band shell and then stop somewhere for lunch. His eyes lit up. He hadn't been on a field trip in quite a while. Nat was just as excited. About twenty-some minutes later they pulled up into the parking lot of the park. They both got out. She just happened to have her digital camera in the backseat, and took time to pull it out. They walked up to the band shell. Nat was in awe of the detail. She didn't know much about architecture, but she knew it was an amazing piece of art. She had Carson stand in front of his design and took several photos. She had a feeling that with the expression of his face, and the beautiful backdrop, the photos were extra special. She would need to make sure his family in Michigan received a copy.

The next morning Nat was at CLC enjoying a coffee and fresh out-of-the oven white chocolate raspberry scone. She was savoring every bite and enjoying every sip of her coffee. Her taste buds seemed more alive than usual. She felt a little swing in her step. Her field trip with Carson was therapeutic for both of them. She had grabbed the local newspaper from the rack, thankful she didn't have to spend the money to subscribe. While reading the paper she noticed a photography contest, with the subject being people. The next day she sought out Carson and asked for his permission to enter the photo she took of him standing next to his band shell design. He told her to go for it.

Six

It was a Friday night and Nat had the decaf brewing and an oatmeal cake in the oven. She rarely baked anymore, but oatmeal cake with brown sugar and coconut topping sounded oh so good. It was close to that time of night when her younger brother, Bryce, would send the weekly text message of "have a good weekend." Nat had just taken the cake out of the oven, when she heard the incoming ding from her cell phone. Like clockwork, was the message, and like clockwork the text was quickly followed up with a response from her sister, Gwen.

A text from Nat would soon follow; she wasn't one to carry her cell phone with her from room to room. The three of them would keep the string of texts alive for at least thirty minutes. When the question was posed to Nat on how she was doing, her response would always be "fine," although not always the case. She had her moments but figured people would tire of her, if she responded honestly. Nat was known for her text responses not making sense at times. She had the habit of hitting the wrong key, aka "fat fingering". After thirty minutes her entire sentences would not make sense, hence the usual cut-off time. She would end the text conversation with reminders not to use the cell phone while behind the wheel. She often wondered if people were tired of her reminders.

The next morning was going to be an extra special one at CLC. One of Elsie's former customers was moving into an assisted living apartment and had no room for his baby grand piano. He gave it to Elsie, who thought it would get more use at CLC rather than her small home. The piano was en route to CLC, compliments of *YOUR BECK*

AND CALL MOVERS, a local moving company. Well, perhaps the move wasn't totally complimentary—she had promised the movers free coffee for a year.

Little did Elsie know, she had a musical superstar in her coffee shop, and the use of the piano would go a long way. Sid was musically gifted, when it came to playing the piano. His mother had bought a keyboard at a garage sale when Sid was ten, and he made good use of it. He was fortunate as the school had a mentor program, and his mentor just happened to teach piano. No one was more excited than Sid for this elegant fixture at CLC. He couldn't wait to try it out.

Elsie sensed Sid was musically inclined. Most times he looked like he was playing a song in his head. She invited him to be the first person to play. He started to play Elton John's, "Your Song." After a few bars, everyone was in awe. Sid played with feeling and emotion. After he was done all the customers cheered and clapped. There wasn't a dry eye in the house. Sid rose from the piano bench and took a bow. He was gleaming.

"Well, I sure appreciated the opportunity to be the first one to play a song at CLC," said Sid, as he looked at Elsie. Elsie and the rest of the customers' mouths were wide open, so much so each could catch a fly, had there been flies in CLC, which was very unlikely.

"You'll have to play for the Card Club guys next week," Elsie said proudly as she gave Sid a pat on his shoulder. "You're full of surprises. Your family must be so proud of you."

Little did Elsie know, Sid's home life was challenging at times. His father left when Sid was five years old. Sid only had a few blip memories of him. His mother struggled to make ends meet. She served in the army for a few years after high school. Her health insurance benefit from the VA was a big help.

"Say, Elsie," said Nat in an excited voice. "I have an idea I want to run past you. My very first 45 LP record was Elton's 'Your Song.' How about I have it framed and we hang it on the wall by the piano? It would be like a commemorative display. We could have a little gold plaque with Sid being the first one to play the piano at CLC. What do you think?" Elsie thought it was a wonderful idea. In fact, her visionary skills immediately went to work.

"Wait a minute, wait a minute," said Elsie as a sketch was coming to mind. "I have an idea." She envisioned having the piano on a small stage along the back wall with a chandelier centered over the piano, and a candelabra on top of the piano. She got so excited at the thought she couldn't think straight. She knew she could rely on the expertise of the Card Club crew. Her plan was to put their skills to good use, and she thought they'd enjoy being part of the project.

The following week when the Card Club crew was gathered, Elsie asked Sid to play. They were amazed. The men gladly volunteered to head up the project and see it through. Every now and then one would get on the other's nerves, but, for the most part, they worked well together. Elsie asked Nat to keep an eye out for a chandelier and candelabra. Being an estate sale and garage sale enthusiast, it didn't take long before several treasures had a home at CLC. Nat was fond of the saying "one person's junk is another's treasure." Within two weeks there was a mini-stage, with the necessary accents. The last final detail of the Card Club crew was adhering the gold plaque to a wall on the stage. It read: "This stage is dedicated to Arthur Jones, who graciously donated the piano, and also to Sid King, who played the first song on it, under the CLC roof on May 28, 2016."

During Sid's breaks he'd play the piano. It was like a free concert to those at CLC. Customers would pull up sheet music on their iPads and tablets. Sid could play just about anything. CLC's business was booming. It was always busy, and now to the extent where more staff was needed. Elsie mentioned on more than one occasion to her staff that she would need to advertise for more workers. Sid asked Elsie if she'd consider hiring his mother, Grace. He gave Elsie a rundown on her cooking and baking skills. He said she ran a tight ship, as she served as a cook in the army. Elsie was thrilled at the idea and asked him to have his mother report the next day, if it worked with her schedule. Grace started the next day and more than fulfilled Elsie's expectations. So much so that Grace became a permanent full-time employee. It was a win-win for both women. Elsie soon realized where Sid's work ethic came from. The apple didn't fall far from Grace's tree.

Elsie's master plan was to create a sense of community. She wanted CLC to be more than an ordinary coffee shop. The mini-stage with the piano was a start. She wanted something to involve the young and old. She always had a few books and toys for the very young, but wanted to give that area a little facelift. She declared that area as Kid's Corner. She enlisted Nat's help with finding a few pieces, including a red wagon to store the books, and some colorful artwork. Also in her schematic plan was a room for teens, seniors, and in-between to hang out and shoot the breeze. She would provide two laptop computers and a printer for her customers to use. She thought that such a room would get the young and old engaged. Her plan included enough space to hold fourteen people. She coined that room "THE HANGOUT ROOM." She would once again enlist the help of the Card Club crew to plan and build the room.

She took it a step further with lining up guest speakers. She coined the speaking engagements "THIS AND THAT CHATS." It wasn't long before she booked the first THIS AND THAT CHAT speaker—Krista McAnders, Jake's sister. The topic near and dear to Krista, was bullying. Krista was scheduled to speak on Friday, July 15 at 7:00 pm. Harlan and Kelly also signed up to present.

June had arrived. The Card Club crew were excited with the thought of assisting Elsie with THE HANGOUT ROOM. Their goal was to finish the room in six weeks. Elsie promised them free coffee and food while they worked. One afternoon one of the teen customers, Anthony, happened to eye the hand-drawn sketch work of Carson.

Carson was sitting at a table closest to the counter, where he could get easy access to coffee refills. Anthony leaned over and asked Carson why he didn't use a computer to draw out the plan. Carson said the only thing he used a computer for was to email his daughter and her family. He didn't want to buy one of those fancy programs and learn it at his age. He said he was told his computer didn't have enough gigs and memory—or something like that.

Anthony acknowledged that it made sense. He happened to have an interest in architecture, as well, and planned to major in that field. Carson challenged Anthony to come up with a drawing for THE HANGOUT ROOM by the next afternoon. The plan was to meet at 3:30, at the same table and present their final sketch. They had an appreciation for each other's work. Carson even picked up on a few techy words. From then on when they saw each other, they had something to talk about. They saw each other often at CLC and always made time to chat.

Elsie got to know Anthony, and asked for his assistance in picking out two laptops, and a printer for THE HANGOUT ROOM. He was thrilled to offer advice, and said how so many customers would appreciate access to the laptops and printer. The Card Club crew used the laptops often to Skype with their families who lived far away. On occasion they would ask the teen whippersnappers for assistance, and the whippersnappers were happy to help.

Seven

Both Jake and Harlan were regular customers at CLC and had been for years. But their paths never crossed. Jake was there mornings, except Sundays, and Harlan was there on Monday and Thursday afternoons to play cards. Elsie got wind that the Card Club schedule was changing to early mornings—at least for two months. One of the Card Club crew had physical therapy appointments a few blocks away and didn't want to make two trips to the area in one day.

"Hey Jake, can you spare a minute?" asked Elsie.

"Sure. You look like a cat that swallowed a mouse," said Jake with a guarded voice and suspicious eyes.

"Wish it were that easy," said Elsie as they walked to a corner for some privacy.

"Sid!" shouted Elsie, as she motioned him to cover the front counter, as many times before. "I'd like you to cover me for a minute please."

"Jake, I wanted to let you know you may be bumping into Harlan. He's been a customer here ever since I opened. You haven't crossed paths because of your schedules. Now his schedule is changing, and he will be here the same time as you, at least for two months. Has something to do with one of the Card Club guy's physical therapy appointment switching to mornings, and the physical therapy office is two blocks away. It's too much for his wife to make two trips to this neck of the woods in one day."

"I appreciate the heads up," said Jake, as he was at a loss for words. "I'll be fine. It's about time I had a chat with Harlan. I know he wishes he could turn back the clock, and heard he has issues with depression. I don't plan on changing my schedule. The first time seeing each other may be somewhat uncomfortable, but we'll get through it." Jake appreciated knowing in advance that there might be an uncomfortable situation on the horizon.

Shortly after Elsie went back to cover the front counter, she received a call from Nat. Nat explained that she was at a multi-family garage sale and came across a red wagon for the Kid's Corner. Nat found other treasures as well but had to use some restraint. Nat took the wagon home to clean before delivering to CLC. She figured that wagon must have been over fifty years old. There were three sets of initials carved on it—HM, JM, and MM. The people holding the garage sale told Nat that the wagon ended up in their yard a while back, and had no idea who it belonged to. They asked around the neighborhood but no one knew. Since so much time had passed they decided it was time to let go of it as they had no use for it.

The next morning Nat delivered the wagon to Elsie. Elsie loved it and placed it in the newly renovated Kid's Corner. Elsie did away with the white plastic bins that once held the books. The books were now placed in the wagon.

Nat noticed from a distance that Kelly was working at the front counter. Kelly had waited on Nat a few times, and although there was a certain amount of tension in the air, the interactions went well. However, this time, through Kelly's expression, it seemed as though she wanted to relay some kind of message. Nat followed her instincts and went up to the front counter and ordered an iced tea. Kelly didn't know quite how to initiate the conversation. She wanted to confirm that Nat knew Tanner's last words.

"Here's your iced tea, Mrs. Carter." Kelly's hand shook uncontrollably, as she placed the tea on the counter. If a pin had fallen to the floor it would have been heard. Customers, familiar with the situation, stared at the two. Kelly could sense it. She had more to say— she wasn't quite ready to end the conversation.

"Kelly," said Nat as she was digging through her full purse, "I understand you will be attending college in the fall and majoring in hotel and restaurant management. I wish you the best." Nat didn't want it on her conscious that a bright young woman couldn't concentrate or move forward with life due to a lapse in judgment.

"Mrs. Carter, can you spare a moment?" whispered Kelly.

"Sure," said Nat, not knowing what other choice there was, but also realized it must have took strength on Kelly's part to ask.

Without hesitation Elsie, having overheard Nat and Kelly's exchange, quickly covered the front counter. Kelly shared with Nat the events of the accident and how terrible she felt. But there may have been one request from Tanner left undone. For Tanner's sake Kelly wanted to make sure that no stone was left unturned. Kelly skipped to the part after she had missed the stop sign and struck Tanner on the motorcycle. She immediately called 911 and the ambulance was there in about five minutes. She recalled that Tanner was conscious, and seemed to be concerned about his condition. He asked the attending paramedic to tell his family how much he loved them and to make sure a message got to his wife—no matter how strange it sounded. He said, "Tell my wife 'You're still wrong.'" Kelly observed the paramedic and knew he had no time to document that statement. Their first and foremost priority was to get Tanner stabilized.

"Kelly," said Nat, "Let me get this straight. You're telling me Tanner's last words to be relayed to me were 'You're still wrong?'"

"Yes, Mrs. Carter. I might have misunderstood, but I'm pretty sure those were his words."

Nat burst into laughter and tears streamed down her face. Kelly seemed perplexed. Elsie was dying to know what was being discussed. She couldn't imagine what could be so funny, especially between the two of them. Nat couldn't stop laughing. She thought no one would ever understand the significance of those words but herself—and Tanner. Tanner had the last words! *That little shit*, thought Nat. Knowing those were his last words brought Nat so much joy. Those words are what Tanner really would have wanted Nat to hear. Those words were better than "I love you."

"Kelly, I can't tell you how much it means to me that you went out of your comfort zone to share this with me. It must not have been easy. You must think I'm crazy, because I laughed so hard. There is a story behind those words. Years ago Tanner and I had a disagreement, and I don't even recall what it was about. Must have been about something stupid. Well, he wrote 'You're still wrong' on a piece of paper and made dozens of copies—sticking in drawers, my vehicle, and so many other places." Nat started to laugh again, shaking her head. Soon both Nat and Kelly were laughing and crying, and the customers were wondering what was going on.

Suddenly all seemed so much better with Nat's world. Learning Tanner's last words, the background chatter, and laughter, Sid taking a moment to play a song, and the aroma of a CLC special made Nat feel alive. It appeared as though Kelly felt some relief, like she had done Tanner a favor, which she actually did. She felt like a weight had been lifted from her shoulders. Nat wished she could have relayed a message of forgiveness to Kelly, but she wasn't at that point, not yet.

Like clockwork, Jake was at CLC and ordered the usual. After he picked up his order he sat in his usual spot, which was close to Kid's Corner. He began, per usual, to check emails on his phone. He put his phone down, and, as he started to pull apart the raspberry scone, the red wagon placed nine feet away caught his eye.

It couldn't be ... what are the chances? he thought. He put down his scone and walked over to the wagon. He looked on the back end of it and noticed the three sets of initials. He experienced a wave of sadness, shortly replaced with a wave of comfort.

When Elsie walked past him to go see if the Card Club crew needed anything, Jake motioned her to stop over to his table. He explained the history of the wagon and wondered where she found it. She explained that Nat picked it up at a local garage sale. She apologized if the presence of the wagon caused painful memories. He explained that it was meant to be. It made him feel like Matthew was there. He also added that he had two of Matthew's favorite books at home and would add to Elsie's collection. He said Matthew's favorite books were *Green Eggs and Ham,* and *Peanut the Wandering Elephant.*

Elsie always felt uneasy about asking Jake how Lisa, his former wife, was doing. But something made her finally ask. Jake explained that she still attended a grief support group, and is actually providing support to people, who recently lost a loved one. She has been free of sedatives for a few months, and was looking and acting better. He was extremely disheartened at the physician who kept prescribing zombie drugs. Jake assumed the physician didn't have any tricks left in his bag. He was glad that Prince's death created an awareness of over-prescribing, among other things. Jake thanked Elsie for her concern.

He sat back down and was finishing up his coffee and scone when he noticed Harlan had entered CLC. Their eyes met. For a few seconds, Harlan had frozen like a deer caught in headlights, and then performed a fast pivot, exiting CLC. A morning storm was on the horizon. It was thundering and lightning. Dorothy, who had dropped him off, had already left. Jake made a dash for the door and calmly asked Harlan to come inside and talk for a few minutes. Harlan nodded. The expression on his face was blank.

"Harlan, it has been a long time since we spoke," said Jake as he tried to compose himself and think of what to say. "I really don't know what to say except nothing is going to bring Matthew back to us. Matthew looked up to you and I know that he wouldn't want you to spend the rest of your life in turmoil, and, frankly, neither do I. I understand you have finished your community service and plan to continue with educating others. It brings some comfort knowing that you are doing all you can. Lisa mentioned that she heard through the grapevine about your presentations and there is chatter—in a good way. Keep it up."

Harlan had a hard time getting words to come out of his mouth. Jake had told him to take his time. As Harlan was ready to say something, the corner of his eye caught the red wagon, and tears followed. Jake realized it was tough for Harlan to see, and made it easy on him by saying the wagon should help them remember the good times.

"Harlan, why don't you join your Card Club buddies, and I'll catch you another time. Please give my best to Dorothy."

Jake wanted to be able to express words of forgiveness to Harlan. He wasn't quite there yet, but perhaps in time. Jake came to realize that not only did Harlan get a sentence of 100 hours of community service, but he was also sentenced to a lifetime of guilt.

As Jake was making his way out of CLC, he mentioned to Elsie that his visit to CLC had been full of surprises—in a good way. He spoke too soon about good surprises. As he exited CLC, a robin flew over him, dropping a wet and gooey surprise on his shoulder. He realized it was only a matter of time, and now gave serious consideration to Nat's practice of using an umbrella upon entering and exiting CLC.

Eight

July had arrived with humid vengeance. Elsie was hoping the A/C would hold out. THE HANGOUT ROOM was finished two days prior to the first ever THIS AND THAT CHAT engagement. Krista McAnders and Harlan Hansen had been slated for the July schedule.

It was 6:45 pm on July 15, and Krista got to CLC a little early to grab an iced tea. She had short brown hair with beautiful highlights, a creamy complexion, and dressed casually, but with class. Her plan was to pick up a sea salt caramel brownie after she finished her gig—a little treat to herself. To her surprise, there were eleven teens who showed up, and a few parents. She welcomed them and started out by saying she does not have a degree in psychology, but can speak to bullying from her personal experience. She displayed confidence, and immediately captured the attention of her audience.

She began by sharing her first recounts of being bullied. She was around twelve years old. She gave a description of how she viewed herself, and commented that her low self-esteem might have contributed to her being an easy target. The description: shy, frail, pale, ample zits, large gap between her two front teeth, and no athletic ability. She dreaded the Presidential Physical Fitness Test. She'd lose sleep at the thought of it. Not only was she picked on at school, but also by some of the neighbor kids.

Things turned around by the time she was sixteen. She started making trips to the library and reading up on self-improvement and how to gain confidence. What sealed the deal was an article in a magazine geared towards teenage girls. There was an article where a teen had shared her story almost identical to Krista's. Also in the same issue were tips on how to apply makeup, and easy-to-do hairstyles. She made a visit to the local pharmacist and asked for his opinion on how to tackle pimples. He made two suggestions: First, he said never touch your face with your hands, followed by a short lecture on how hands are full of bacteria. Then he asked her if she drank lots of cola products, which she did. He suggested she cut down on cola. Over the course of a week there were signs of improvement in the tackle pimple project. Little by little she started to gain self-confidence, and started to speak up. When someone would pick on her she would bluntly ask them why they were being such a pain. She wouldn't allow herself to be a doormat and she called people on their rudeness. She finally realized that no one is exempt from bullying. Not even adults.

"As an observer on Facebook, adult bullying seems to have reared its ugly head, being easier to do than ever before," she said. There are helpful tools on the Internet. During my bullying days, it seemed as though schools didn't do much to stop it. Some school officials passed it off as part of life. Lucky for you things are changing and there is awareness. Bullies are getting a bad reputation. Some tend to be self-proclaimed rulers who get a natural high from being in control. Keep in mind they may have issues you are not aware of. They may have demanding, pushy parents, and their outlet may be to find a host, just like a virus does."

Krista wrapped up her chat by telling her small audience that she had attended two years of community college. Her parents didn't have the financial means to help her and her brother, Jake, with college. She added that the two years of post-high school education and on-the-job training served her well. She had an eye for fashion, and sales. With the assistance of the Small Business Association, and other resources, she was able to start up her own business.

By the age of thirty-five she owned several successful boutiques. Although she was financially sound, she reminded the group that success should be based on happiness, not title or financial status. She shared a little side note: Once financially sound at the age of thirty-five, she treated herself to braces. In her younger days she kept a list of models who kept true to themselves and left the tooth gap, many became famous for it, so if she never had braces, that would have been okay too.

When she ended her chat, there was clapping, and lots of discussion. She was asked by some of the teens to come back and share her story again. She said she'd be honored and thanked them for coming.

A week passed. Harlan was on the schedule for his THIS AND THAT CHAT. He was a little nervous thinking Jake might attend. Jake was there but out of sight. He stood in the next room, being within listening distance. There were nine attendees. Dorothy attended each of Harlan's speaking engagements. Harlan began with stating that he wasn't there to preach, but to share what he had learned, and the heartache he and others have endured.

"Giving up the keys shouldn't be based on age, but physical and mental health," Harlan said. "Heck, a forty-year-old may have impairment issues and should give up keys. Typically our bodies are usually wearing out more after a certain age. You know your body. What does it tell you? If you are taking long naps, perhaps you should reconsider the drive to snowbird land. In a way, giving up your keys is giving up some of your independence. But if you seriously injure or kill someone, what kind of independence is that?"

At the conclusion of his talk, he asked the attendees to take notice of the little red wagon in the Kid's Corner. He shared the memories of Matthew's wagon, recounting the day he helped fix a squeaky wheel. "There were three sets of initials carved in the wagon— three generations," said Harlan with a noticeable lump in his throat. "You don't want to be in my shoes and feel a pit in your stomach every day at 3:48 pm, the time of the accident. At some point our driving privilege will be gone; it's a painful reality. Listen to the voice inside you, and your family and friends. Think long and hard."

Although many of the attendees didn't think giving up the keys applied to them at this point in time, it made them think. And if they did, that was all Harlan could ask for.

THIS AND THAT CHATs took off. It created a buzz, and many community members, although a tight squeeze, took advantage of the free space.

Kelly was scheduled to present at THIS AND THAT CHAT in late August before heading to college.

It was another hot and humid day in the latter part of July. Elsie waited for the line to dwindle before she would take a break. Around 9:00 am, she got her chance. She helped herself to a chair at Nat's table. Nat always welcomed the company. Elsie was known for offering unsolicited information.

Out of the blue she started to deliver the story on Jake's life. She said that Jake had been married for ten years but the death of Matthew took a toll on the marriage. His wife, Lisa, had, for a brief period, turned to sedatives. Jake stood by her side during treatment, but they had grown apart. Lisa seemed stronger and developed coping skills, but was no longer able to remain in the relationship as his wife. Although their marriage had ended at her request, they remained friends. Jake visits her now and then, and lends a helping hand when needed. Nat thought losing a husband after twenty-seven years of marriage was hard enough, but couldn't imagine the loss of a child.

Nine

August had arrived, and people from the upper Midwest usually relished the heat, as they knew what was around the corner. It's a popular time for outdoor gatherings and trips, which in Nat's case included a family reunion on Tanner's side. Nat had just pulled up to the local grocery store. As she was getting out, the wind took the door of her SUV and missed hitting some fancy vehicle by a hair. She grabbed the door in a nick of time. "Crap," she mumbled while thinking what a close call it was. Her hand was nearly pinned between her door and the door of the Porsche. She's glad she didn't have to explain a dent to its owner.

She focused on her assignment of bringing pasta salad to the family reunion. The reunion was the following day, and this would be the first family reunion without Tanner. But, by hell or high water, she was going to get through it. She was glad that her daughters, and their special friends, Josh and Chet, would be joining her on the road trip to Stockholm, Wisconsin. One of Tanner's relatives organized the reunion, and Stockholm was the best in-between meeting spot that had a beautiful park with a charming pavilion. Nat was hoping there was some kind of shelter should severe weather approach. She was known as THE NERVOUS NAT when it came to stormy weather. She had declared herself as an honorary weather person, and was slightly annoying at times when sending text messages to family members when storms were in the forecast. Most storms never panned out.

The crew was on the road by 9:48 am the next morning. Nat was a stickler for time—always down to the minute. The trip from

Stone Creek to Stockholm took about two hours. The gathering time for the reunion was noon. They wanted to allow time to stop and stretch their legs, and grab a beverage.

They made it to the City of Stockholm pavilion at noon on the dot. Relatives acknowledged their arrival, as they pulled up. Tanner's parents and sister, Kathy, greeted the crew as they got out of the SUV. Laughs and tears followed long hugs. Nat and her girls already felt a sense of relief, and a bundle of love.

"We're sure glad you could all make it," said Tanner's dad with a chipper voice. "Been too long since we've seen you." Tanner's mother and sister echoed in agreement.

"I know. I plead guilty," said Nat. "The only excuse is that I'm not one for being stuck in a vehicle for more than an hour, but that's nothing new to you. Not sure if this old dog will ever change."

There was the usual fare of grilled burgers and brats, potato salad, chips, cookies, bars, soda, iced tea, coffee, and, of course, cold beer—regular and near beer. Nat placed her contribution of pasta salad on a long table with the rest of the food. She used the same recipe Tanner used. It was a hit. Many of Tanner's relatives had brought photo albums. It was nice to actually look at photo albums, which seem to be close to extinction these days. Also entertaining was the usual bean bag toss game, which was Sarah and Sadie's favorite outdoor game.

It was good to reminisce the many stories. It was also comforting to hear laughter. There was nothing uncomfortable in any way, shape, or form. It felt like Tanner was there.

Nat kept her eye on her cell phone weather app. Storms were expected to hit around 7:00 pm. Her plan was to make time to make a pit stop to Alma, Wisconsin, which was thirty miles south of Stockholm.

Tanner had once shown her a scenic overlook located at Buena Vista Park in Alma. It was one of his favorite spots. She wanted to share this spot as a suggestion to scatter his ashes. Being Nervous Nat, she wanted to leave Stockholm by 2:45 on the dot to allow enough time. She gave the usual "let's go" signal to Sarah and Sadie. Josh and Chet had come to know the "let's go" signal as well.

They thought Nat was a bit like a drill sergeant, but overlooked it. She was good to them so it was hard for them to be too annoyed. Nat and crew said their good-byes to everyone and thanked them for a memorable time, and extended an invitation to drive up and visit them sometime. Tanner's sister, an avid Packer fan, said she'd be in touch with an invitation to a Packer vs. Viking party. Kathy was known for hosting fun and creative parties. She always had enough food to feed an army. Nat replied to her saying that she looked forward to the party, and would be wearing purple in order to neutralize all the green.

Nat asked Chet to use his cell phone for driving directions to Buena Vista Park. Just like the GPS maps indicated, it was a thirty-minute drive, and it went by fast. It was a short distance from the parking lot to the overlook. They were in awe of the beauty.

"Girls," said Nat. What do you think of this place to release your Dad's ashes?" Both girls thought it was the perfect place. They decided to make a road trip in the spring.

The following Monday afternoon, Jake made an unplanned stop at CLC. He needed to find a congratulations card for a co-worker. He happened to overhear some of the high schoolers talk about which global positioning system phone app was better. Jake was wondering if any of them had ever used a regular road map. He had a funny feeling the answer was no. He joined in on the conversation and received some odd looks, like he was from the dinosaur times. Jake went out to his vehicle and grabbed a Rand McNally map. He placed it on the table and suggested the group try it. He encouraged them to play THE MAP GAME. He said using the cell phone's apps are convenient, but thought they might enjoy the challenge of a paper map.

The next week when they saw Jake they thanked him for the suggestion. They had a good time with it. They realized it would be good to have a map should their cell phone battery die.

It was the last Wednesday in August. Kelly had scheduled her THIS AND THAT CHAT a few days prior to her heading to college. She was slightly more nervous than usual. She was concerned that Nat might attend. Nat did attend but kept out of sight—just close enough to listen. The seats were filled and some people had to stand. Kelly began her chat with statistics. She figured most have heard the stats before, but the stats of deaths and accidents caused by distracted driving had grown and she thought it was worth the mention.

She mentioned that Mothers Against Drunk Driving had been around for decades and asked who was to lead the other version of MADD—Mothers Against Distracted Driving. One is as bad as the other. She limited the "statistics" conversation and got to the part how one moment of sending a text created a lifetime of heartache for so many people. She shared her continued panic attacks and flashbacks. She shared how the associated costs with the accident set her folk's retirement back by several years. Her folks were hard workers and put money aside to travel, and now that wouldn't happen for a while.

"I really messed up," she said. "And it can easily happen to any of you. Please note that distracted driving isn't a teen epidemic—it applies to everyone behind the wheel. It not only applies to texting but using your phone for a conversation as well. I hope you'll share my example with others. I can't do it alone. Thank you for coming."

There was lots of discussion after she finished her chat. Nat quickly ran out the front door before being seen by Kelly. Elsie noticed the quick escape. Before Kelly left CLC, Elsie had mentioned how proud she was. Kelly promised that she would give her THIS AND THAT CHAT at every opportunity. Meanwhile, Nat had arrived home. She thought about what Kelly had said, and burst into a good cry.

Ten

It was the first Saturday in September, and there was already a touch of fall in the air. Kelly was at college in Menomonie, Wisconsin. She planned to work at CLC during the holidays and an occasional weekend. Sid was now a senior and still applying to colleges. He could only go to college if it was on a full scholarship. He was hoping for a music scholarship.

It was around 1:00 pm when Elsie left CLC to stretch her legs and get some fresh air. Her plan was to be back in thirty minutes. Forty minutes later Nat received a call from Elsie saying she was in the emergency room. She had fallen when stepping down from a curb at the park. She had a fractured tibia, which required surgery. She'd be out of commission for two months. She was concerned about keeping CLC running. Nat assured Elsie things would work out. She would get some volunteers to help.

The Card Club guys, and their wives came to mind. Of course there had to be proper training. The hardest part would be teaching a few people how to work the cash register. Harlan's wife, Dorothy, was the expert when it came to making egg coffee. She was the head of the funeral committee at her church and had been making egg coffee for decades. Sid's mother, Grace, was in charge of all the baked goods. Elsie extended her appreciation and said she'd stop by in a few days to answer questions, but would need to stay off her feet. Her signing up for rides to medical appointments came much earlier than she ever expected.

Shortly after Elsie's fall all was pretty much under control, but more help would make it easier. Chuck, Nat's handyman, had finished his substance abuse treatment program and called Nat to let her know he was, once again, available for odd jobs.

"Chuck," said Nat with relief. "Your timing is perfect. First, I'm glad you finished treatment and wish you the best. Second, I have an unusual proposal. By any chance are you interested in working at CLC? Elsie, the owner had an accident and is out of commission for two months. I'm trying to round up volunteers and some paid staff until she gets back in full force. She pays pretty well, and you'd have unlimited free coffee while you work. I can't say for sure but I have a funny feeling this might turn into a full-time position, given how crazy busy this place is."

"You sold me," he said, happy to feel needed again. Chuck reported for work the following day. He easily caught on to how things operated. Elsie was making frequent appearances, which was appreciated by her volunteers and staff. She soon realized that a procedure manual would be beneficial, and that was something that could be worked on at home. She was off pain medication and no longer felt like she was in the twilight zone. She started to take ibuprofen, and put her pain meds in a safe place until she could safely dispose of them. She often wondered why her local pharmacy didn't have a prescription disposal drop-off, like some police stations do.

Saturday, September 17 had arrived. Sarah and Sadie were pleased with the display in the party room, and all the other preparations.

Nat had treated herself to a pair of shiny red flats. She had a love for shoes and purses. She wore black leggings, a long red and black poncho, and the silver dangling earrings Tanner had given her on their twentieth wedding anniversary. Before she headed to the party she listened to one of his voicemails she had saved. Every year he would sing happy birthday to her—in a sexy voice.

"Wish you were here, Tanner," talking to herself again. "Sorry you're missing out on the fun, but I'll have a toast to you. You may be gone, but you'll never be forgotten. I just came across some of your popcorn remnants in the couch. I have a funny feeling there are more."

Nat arrived to the party room at Sadie's apartment complex shortly before 6:00 pm. The room was absolutely beautiful, and decorated with mini-lantern lights. She noticed a baby grand piano in the corner, and upon further examination saw Sid sitting at the piano bench. He was hired to play. He told Sarah and Sadie he'd play for free, but they insisted on paying him. Besides, they told him, when he becomes famous they can say he played at their mother's party.

Sid's mother, Grace, had been hired to cater the party. This was her first paid catering job. She had prepared cocktail meatballs, chicken wings, pigs in a blanket, pastry-wrapped brie, and a fruit tray, as well as a variety of fancy cupcakes. Dorothy was in the kitchen watching over the egg coffee. There was also wine and beer. Grace's culinary talents were a hit. Little did she know that within a few months she would be running her own part-time catering business. She would continue to work at CLC, because she enjoyed the customers and sense of belonging.

Elsie and Jake arrived shortly after Nat. Nat was pleasantly surprised, but shocked to see Jake. She walked over and greeted them. She hugged Elsie.

"Nat, I asked Jake if he'd be my date, as I didn't want to miss your party. I know your girls have been working hard to make it perfect. By the looks of things, it appears it is," said Elsie, as she fidgeted with her motorized scooter. "Chuck is covering CLC tonight, bless his heart. I'll treat him to a fancy dinner to make up for it."

"Jake, I'm thrilled that you escorted Elsie, and Elsie, thanks for telling me that Chuck is covering CLC. I owe him a plate of chocolate sour cream cookies," said Nat.

"The pleasure is all mine," said Jake with longer than usual eye contact. "And I agree with Elsie—it looks as though your daughters could go into the party planning business."

Jake saw Dorothy and Harlan from a distance and gave a wave, and smile. To avoid any awkwardness, he thought he'd give them their space and talk face-to-face with them another time. People started arriving—more than Nat had expected. The guest list was to be short, but the girls invited some of Nat's friends from her hometown, and Tanner's friends from his hometown. The mix of guests celebrating a happy occasion hadn't been like that since Tanner and Nat's wedding. There were laughs, tears, and lots of references to "remember when." A noticeably appreciated background sound was Sid at the piano. Sarah and Sadie had a few requests, but left the rest up to Sid. He knew what kind of music Nat enjoyed. The night flew by, and, as promised, the girls had put an end time to the party. Guests gave Nat hugs, as they left. This time Jake had leaned over and gave Nat a hug as well.

"I'm sure I'll see you at CLC soon," he said to Nat, as he helped Elsie with her coat and scooter. "It was a great party. I don't even know most of your guests but nevertheless had a fun time."

As usual, Nat and Jake saw each other at CLC. They both continued to volunteer at CLC until Elsie proved she was ready to run the show again. When not on duty, Jake seemed glued to his phone, and Nat seemed to hide behind a newspaper or the greeting card rack. They would acknowledge each other with a smile, and small talk. Yet both had an inkling that there might be more than just coffee brewing. Inconspicuous peeks at each other were a common occurrence. For some reason neither was quite ready to propose something more than small talk. It would most likely take 'An Act of Elsie' to get this special brew started. The weekend after Nat's party, Elsie came to CLC to observe. What was to be an hour's stay ended up being five hours. She missed working.

It was early November, and Elsie was back at work part-time. She continued to enlist the help of others. Her fall had taken the wind out of her sail, and returning full time would be a while longer.

One day she noticed Jake was hanging around longer than usual. Her intuition told her he wanted to talk. She pretended to straighten up the Kid's Corner, giving him an opportunity to approach her.

"Elsie, so what is the story with Nat?" he asked not knowing if he was going too far with his curiosity.

"Well, she lost her husband, Tanner, over a year ago. Motorcycle accident. Sensitive subject around here as our Kelly is the one who hit him. Error in judgment, and she's paying for it. Ever since, Nat has been like a rabbit in a rabbit hole, with CLC being the rabbit hole. She and Tanner would spend Saturday mornings here, but since he passed she spends almost every day here. She may appear to be standoffish, but once one gets to know her she lets her guard down. She volunteers, bringing folks to their medical appointments. And, as you saw, she has two beautiful daughters. She has a sister and brother-in-law in Brainerd, and a brother and sister-in-law in San Antonio. Besides photography, she loves to seek out garage sales. I usually have a 'keep your eyes out' list for her. Her parents died a few years ago—days apart. They say her father died of a broken heart. That's all I can think of. Oh, and she loves CLC coffee, if you already didn't know. Yep, that should cover it."

Jake appreciated the thorough run-down. It helped him understand Nat.

One Saturday morning while Elsie was taking a break from the front counter, she noticed that Ed Wright of the *Stone Creek Herald* had entered CLC, and waved to her. She extended the gesture. After Ed was set with his coffee, he pulled up a chair next to Elsie and asked how things were going. As she answered with "amazingly fine," he took a double-take. Kelly, who came home for the weekend to help out, was the only person up front when he came in, but now he saw a crew. He noticed that Nat, Kelly, Harlan, Dorothy, and Jake were working within feet of each other. Kelly at the register, Harlan and Dorothy stocking the front display case with scones and muffins, Jake placing ceramic CLC coffee cups on the shelf, and Nat wiping up crumbs and spills on the front counter.

Ed was amazed at how all of them were working together under such unusual circumstances. "What are the chances?" he thought. He always carried his camera, and with all of their permissions clicked on the shutter button. He now had what he needed for a story.

Ed left to go work on it. He was familiar with the situations. His recollection was that Kelly was not given a sentence of community service, but had her license suspended for a year. At the time of the sentencing, she was in no shape to speak in public. There were both ends of the spectrum. Kelly Henderson, a driver with not much experience behind the wheel, and Harlan Hansen, a driver with decades of experience, but stubborn. Ed realized his story had taken on a new dimension. Not only was it about community service sentences, it was also about voluntary community service.

Elsie was going to hang around a few minutes before asking someone for a ride home. Chuck caught her eye. She noticed what a diligent worker he was, in addition to being genuinely kind and good with customers. She was thankful for his help, and eventually appreciated his companionship, as he with her.

Eleven

Elsie returned to work full time shortly after Thanksgiving, and was thankful to be feeling one hundred percent. She was looking forward to decorating for the holidays. One mild early December morning, Elsie noticed Jake outside, and by his gestures he wasn't a happy camper. Elsie was curious as to what could get Jake so riled up. She went outside pretending to tend to something that needed fixing. She was pretty convincing when she wanted to be. Jake had his cell phone on speaker mode. She could tell he was attempting to speak to a live person. He repeated two words over and over. "CUSTOMER SERVICE, CUSTOMER SERVICE, CUSTOMER SERVICE. No! Not Curtis Shervis! CUSTOMER SERVICE!" After a minute Elsie heard a voice at the other end, and the message, "a customer service representative will be with you shortly." The message was followed by some cheesy music. Jake was shaking his head. As a rule it took a lot to rock Jake, but Internet service companies seem to have a way of turning the mildest mannered people into ogres.

"You say there is not estimated time for the Internet to be back up and running?" asked Jake to the representative.

Elsie was getting chilled so went back into the shop. Jake came in shortly thereafter.

"Hey Jake, anything I can do to help?" asked Elsie. "You look a tad rattled which is not like you."

"You are observant as usual, Elsie. My office downtown is closed for renovation so we are to work from home. My Internet service is down, so I am not able to print off some documents needed to be filed at the courthouse this morning.”

“I see,” Elsie replied empathetically. “I’d let you use the printer in THE HANGOUT ROOM, but this morning I noticed the black cartridge is empty. I am pretty sure I know someone who can get your papers printed in a jiffy.” She grabbed Jake’s arm and led him to the greeting card stand, where she saw Nat a few minutes ago looking at the birthday cards. “Nat, paging Nat Carter, are you still here?” asked Elsie.

Nat leaned over and was surprised by both Elsie and Jake standing inches from her. Elsie explained Jake’s predicament. Without batting an eye Nat said she’d be happy to let Jake use her computer and printer. Within a few minutes Nat and Jake were at her townhome. They removed their boots and coats and made their way down the hall to the bedroom, which was converted into an office. Jake noticed a pair of men’s eyeglasses on the accent table in the hallway. He found it peculiar to see a glass bowl placed upside down to cover the glasses. He didn’t dare ask the story behind it, but had a funny feeling they belonged to her late husband, and that the visual display provided comfort to her.

“Help yourself, Jake,” said Nat, as she pointed to the desk with the computer and printer. Jake logged into his company’s website and within minutes had the papers printed. He noticed some unique photos on the wall and asked who took them. Nat explained that she had, and was a photographer.

“Wow, you certainly have a neat spin on your subjects. It’s like your subjects are speaking to you. Well, I should get down to the courthouse. You’re a lifesaver, Nat.”

“I’d be happy to help if you ever get in a pinch again,” replied Nat, as they walked through the kitchen to the garage.

As they got into her vehicle he mentioned the layout of her kitchen, and commented how a pantry is such a bonus, especially when trying to hide junk at the last minute. She agreed, and thought how glad she was the pantry was no longer used as her crying booth.

Nat dropped Jake off to his vehicle. As he was getting out, he took a long puzzled look at her. He was trying to figure out why some past flame hadn't come around. Or maybe they had, and Elsie hadn't mentioned it. Nat had an errand to run in Chaska, a town a few miles from Stone Creek.

As she drove down Second Avenue, she noticed a sign for an animal rescue shelter. She entertained the idea of getting a dog, but wanted to hold off until spring. She knew if she went inside the shelter now, she wouldn't come out empty-handed. She had a soft spot for dogs.

That afternoon Sid arrived at work and Elsie noticed he was smiling from ear to ear.

"Sid, dear, given the expression on your face and the bounce in your step, I gather you have some news to share?" Sid picked up Elsie and twirled her around.

"I've been accepted and given a full scholarship to St. Olaf College!" Sid said with excitement. "It's like a dream come true."

"This calls for a celebration," said Elsie proudly. "Young man, there was no doubt in my mind about your getting a scholarship. Now get up on the stage, which has been dedicated to you, and play something for us."

Sid did just that. He played like he never played before. He had more confidence than ever. As usual, customers were in awe. Many of them had tears in their eyes. Elsie motioned Sid's mother from the back room, where she was watching over the egg coffee. "Grace, please do me the honor and join your son on the piano bench. I'll watch over the egg coffee."

The following week, Nat was at CLC placing her usual order. She noticed that Elsie came out from the kitchen and was waving something in the air.

"Congratulations, Nat!" said Elsie holding up the front page of the local paper. What a great photo! I wasn't aware you entered the photo contest."

"Say what?" asked Nat with a surprised look. So much time had passed that Nat didn't think there was a chance of winning the contest. Apparently she didn't get the message. She was more than thrilled.

Nat wouldn't be at CLC in the afternoon when Carson planned to play cards with the Card Club crew, but Elsie said she'd make sure Carson saw the paper. By the time he arrived, he was talk of the town. It meant so much to him to be shown in such a light. People started to ask him about his days of being an architect. He enjoyed sharing his stories.

Twelve

"Well, are we all set?" asked Nat, as she put the SUV in drive after Sarah, Sadie, Josh, and Chet buckled up. "Buena Vista Park, here we come. I have your coffee and potty stop all mapped out. I loaded some of Tanner's favorite songs onto a USB drive. I declare this Tanner Carter Day. Yee ha!"

It was a beautiful Saturday in April. They left town around noon, and made one stop in Prescott, Wisconsin to stretch their legs, use the restroom, and grab a beverage. Tanner's urn was buckled in as well. The plan was to scatter Tanner's ashes.

Upon arrival at Buena Vista Park, Nat carefully removed Tanner's urn. They stood as close as they could to the edge of the overlook without risking their lives. "Well, the time has come," said Nat. "We couldn't have a more beautiful day. Sunshine, sixty-five degrees, and a *light* breeze. Okay girls, all three of us need to hold the urn and then, on the count of three, fling it into in the air. Just don't let go of the urn."

The girls acknowledged the instructions, each placing a hand on the urn, and when Nat yelled out the word three, they flung the urn into the air. While the ashes were in mid-air, a sharp wind came from the opposite direction, causing a hiccup in their plan. All three of them spit and sputtered as remnants of ash were all over them. The guys started to laugh, and then laughter from the girls followed. Laughter from the girls was short lived. By the expression on their faces, it was clear that they were not able to say any last words. Their tear-filled eyes said it all. Although they say a good cry is healthy, Nat knew Tanner wouldn't want the ceremonial event turned into a cryfest, so she quickly interjected.

"Okay, okay, this is not how I imagined the little ceremony to go," said Nat with a cough. "I'm sure your father is having the last laugh." She was glad she carried disinfectant wipes in her purse.

"Why don't the four of you make your way to the SUV, and I'll catch up with you in a minute," Nat said, as she wanted a moment alone. "We'll stop a few miles down the road and have a beverage and fried cheese curds."

Nat took in the beautiful view and thought of the time she and Tanner spent at this park. She recalled her nagging while he drove on the winding road to another town. He drove faster than she was comfortable with. The imprint on the passenger floorboard was evidence of her pressing on a non-existent brake.

"Well, Tanner, if I'm going to say a few words to you I better do it fast before tourists show up," whispered Nat. "Hope you are satisfied with the spot we chose for your ashes, although most ended up on our face, and in our hair. As painful as it is, Alfred Lord Tennyson's line "'Tis better to have loved and lost than never to have loved at all" holds true. Funny how two strangers bumping into each other at a Twins' baseball game led to marriage and two awesome daughters. Just wish I could feel your warm body and have an occasional verbal debate. I'll love you forever."

She then walked back to the SUV, and they cranked up the music and found a local tavern that claimed to serve the best deep fried cheese curds.

Nat slept in the next morning. As a rule she was an early riser, but the emotions from the day before tired her out. She brewed some coffee, made blueberry pancakes, read the *Star Tribune*, and then went for a long walk. After her walk she spent a good share of the day learning photo software tricks. She loved experimenting with photos and was amazed at some of the software features. She found it entertaining, and knew it would take more than a few hours to master the program. While sifting through some childhood photos she came across one photo with her sister and brother. It looked like an oldie.

They were in the backseat of the family car, enjoying a root beer float, while in their pajamas. She figured they were in grade school. It was a priceless photo, needing to be scanned and shared. The photo served as a reminder she needed to make a point to visit with siblings and friends more often. *One can't wait for funerals*, she thought.

After Nat was done with sorting through photos, she made her way to the living room where she stored old pictures in a cabinet. As she walked past the accent table in the hallway, she suddenly stopped, made a pivot, and then looked at Tanner's eyeglasses with the clear glass bowl serving as a protector from dust. She took a deep breath and then removed the bowl. She picked up his eyeglasses, held them over her heart, and then found the case for them. She made the decision to donate the eyeglasses, and recalled a Lion's Club eyeglass collection box at the post office. She made a note on her to-do list for the following day.

It was that time of year when garage sales started up, and Elsie's "be on the lookout for this and that" usually filled up a chunk of Nat's time. But now Nat figured Elsie's decorating needs should be pretty much completed, at least until the next project, whatever that may be. With extra time to spare she had given much thought to adopting a rescue dog, and sometime soon would be best, if she were to make the commitment. She hopped on the computer and started to research breeds.

It had been almost a year since Carson and Anthony worked on the plans for THE HANGOUT ROOM. They saw each other often at CLC, and both had become a fixture to each other. It was near the end of April and Anthony was planning to ask Carson if he needed help with yard work. It was a beautiful Saturday morning, and Anthony had just entered CLC when both Elsie and Chuck motioned him to THE HANGOUT ROOM.

"Anthony," said Elsie, "Carson had to move to his daughter's place in Michigan. He's not one for goodbyes. Carson's a sly fox. He asked us to make sure you were made aware of a secret compartment in THE HANGOUT ROOM. He wanted you to find it yourself. We don't even know where it is. Anyway, he said he left a note for you.

Anthony's eyes welled up with tears. "We'll leave you alone and will put the DO NOT DISTURB sign on the door so you have a little time to yourself." Anthony nodded, and Chuck shut the door. Elsie and Chuck went back to work up front—it was getting pretty busy as the garage sale folks made it a point to meet and then map out their route. Anthony was surprised at the thought of a secret compartment. He walked around the room several times before the corner of his eye noticed a small white something in the vent. He removed the vent cover using a Swiss army pocketknife and saw some paper folded up tightly. It read:

> *Dear Anthony,*
>
> *It has been a pleasure to know you. You renewed my faith in young people. I was getting a little depressed until working on THE HANGOUT ROOM project. Exchanging ideas and having consultations put a new spin on things. When you turn my age, I hope you are able to find a young and gifted whippersnapper such as yourself to experience the same. Sorry I didn't say goodbye in person, but I'm afraid I'd cry like a baby. Not that there's anything wrong with crying. I need to move close to my daughter, as I now need an interpreter at my medical visits. I just don't understand why some of those doctors can't speak in layman's terms. It's like a different language. Well, take care, young man.*
>
> *~Carson*

Anthony's tears were followed by a smile and a tightness in his throat. How lucky he was to have met such a neat man. After a few minutes he walked out into the open area of CLC and went to the front counter. He thanked Elsie and Chuck and then ordered a large pineapple smoothie, hoping it would relax his tight throat muscles. By this time some of his classmates arrived, and they went to THE HANGOUT ROOM to discuss a class project.

"Hey Anthony, make sure you don't share that secret compartment with anyone else. It's yours. Just make sure you don't ever put any wild weed in it, if you know what I mean," Elsie said with a wink and a smile.

"No worries," he responded. "Not my kind of thing. I need a clear head."

Ed entered CLC, with a nearly completed story of the least likely people to work together. He asked Elsie if she'd mind reviewing it. She didn't mind at all.

"Wow, wow," she said as she pulled a tissue from her pocket. "Stone Creek residents better stock up on tissue. Beautifully written, Ed. Very touching, and personal accounts from all sides was a good idea."

Ed had interviewed Jake and his former wife, Harlan, Dorothy, Nat, Sarah, Sadie, Kelly, Kelly's parents, and several others whose lives were sent in a tailspin. The story, entitled "Tragedy Takes a Detour," appeared on the front page, and was well received. He cited Merriam-Webster's definition of detour, which was: "going in a direction that is not planned." It created a buzz, as well as an awareness of responsibilities when behind the wheel. That was all Ed was hoping for.

Thirteen

A few weeks passed. It was early May. Nat was near the finish line of her walking the neighborhood circle. She had mapped her walk, and this time met her goal of four miles. For her, that was something. Years ago she was pleased as punch with walking two miles. She picked up her pace, so she could get the oven turned on and prepare the popover batter as Sarah, Sadie, Josh, and Chet were coming over to be the taste testers of a new recipe. The popovers were to be slathered in hazelnut butter. The girls had also planned to gather up a few old photos to scan, and save to the cloud for safekeeping.

"Mom, what do you have going on tomorrow?" asked Sarah.

"Well, I'm providing medical appointment rides in the morning, and then doing a graduation photo shoot mid-afternoon," said Nat. "But first my usual stop at CLC. Any particular reason you ask?"

It was common for Sarah and Sadie to inquire about their mother's schedule. They were curious as how she kept busy and wondered if she had any interest in someone of the opposite sex. The focus on their mother went in reverse, as they started to sift through the old photos. There were laughs, as they spent a few hours reminiscing. Josh and Chet seemed to be interested in some of the family history. Nat moved the wireless scanner from her office to the kitchen island. She also thought now was a good time as any to save to their favorite photos to a web-based storage place. They could all enjoy them with the ease of a few clicks—that is if they remembered their log-in and passwords.

"Have you ever considered getting a rescue dog to keep you company?" asked Sarah, as she helped herself to a second popover, and acknowledged the recipe was a winner.

"As a matter of fact, I'm keeping my eyes open," said Nat. "Please don't surprise me with a pet like you did with those kittens. Sarah, I don't recall where you found the gray one, but, if memory serves, Sadie found one near the city park. As I recall keeping them lasted less than two days. Although they were adorable, I'm glad you found homes for them. Until then, I never knew I was allergic to cats. My eyes itched for days."

Little did Sarah and Sadie know, Nat had planned to visit the rescue shelter the next morning. Nat had placed a call to the shelter several weeks ago and provided criteria should a dog become available. She wanted a dog that didn't shed and was no taller than 11.5 inches. She was looking at some type of teacup or miniature breed. They contacted her shortly before Sarah and Sadie's visit. Nat didn't want to mention it in case she came home empty-handed.

It was 10:37 pm when the cell phone rang and woke Nat up. It was Hazel stating the garage door was up. "Thanks, Hazel," said Nat with a tone of embarrassment. "I owe you one—*again*. I must sound like a parrot: I owe you one, I owe you one."

The next morning Nat stopped by CLC for her usual fix before heading to the rescue shelter. She wondered if she was doing the right thing. A dog would be good company, but she'd always have to find someone to watch it when she went on trips. Yet, she could always ask either Sarah or Sadie to help out. Nat introduced herself once inside the shelter. The lead volunteer explained there was a miscommunication and the dog she had in mind was already adopted about an hour prior to Nat's arrival.

The volunteer apologized and said there are several other dogs needing to be rescued. Nat shook her head and said she really needed to stick with her specifications. The volunteer understood but thought Nat's use of the word "specifications" made it sound like she was looking for a computer rather than a dog. As Nat made her way to the door she heard a whine, followed by a bark, followed by a yelp. She turned around and saw an Old English Sheepdog. It was huge and hairy. An hour later there was an announcement on Facebook with a photo of Nat's new 90-pound furball companion, named Harry.

Several days later, Nat noticed Harry had a piece of paper between his two front paws and was slobbering like mad. She took a look at the partially chomped paper and noticed it read, "YOU'RE STILL WRONG." Nat burst out into laughter. She thought that she had found all of Tanner's notes.

It had been a little over two years since Tanner's passing. Nat still felt a void, but, little by little, she was moving on. Harry the horse-type dog was a good companion. Nat was forced to take more walks, eventually making new acquaintances, especially at the dog park. Nat had become less and less of a rabbit in the rabbit hole. She reached out to friends she had neglected, and even arranged a few road trips with them.

Nat's persistence with learning the photography software paid off. It took an eye to capture one's subject; it also took skill to produce the final print. Elsie was always interested in taking a look at Nat's photos, especially since many of them were of the Card Club crew. Eventually, several of the Card Club crew photos were framed and hung for all to enjoy. A favorite by many was that of Carson in front of the band shell he'd designed.

It was a beautiful May morning. Jake had picked up his order and taken his seat. As usual he was glued to his cell phone—and had left his credit card on the front counter. Nat entered CLC and shared with Elsie that a friendly bird had dropped a little surprise on her shoulder. She had tossed the "poop umbrella," as people gave her odd looks for using it on sunny days. Jake overheard and chuckled, then went back to his cell phone. Elsie offered to pay for the dry cleaning. Nat wouldn't hear of it. Nat picked up her coffee, scone, and one of the two credit cards on the counter. She glanced down and noticed the name on the card was Jacob C. McAnders. Elsie said that Jake apparently left his card on the counter and asked Nat if she'd deliver it to him.

"Excuse me, Mr. McAnders," said Nat. "I believe this credit card belongs to you. I could have sworn we experienced a similar situation before. Kind of like déjà vu."

"Well now, Ms. Carter, that could very well be a sign that we finally need to arrange a dinner date and get to know each other. Sound like a plan?"

"Sounds like a plan."

Elsie's plan had come to fruition. Church Ladies' Coffee became a community fixture. Other coffee shops tried to replicate CLC, but were not successful. Elsie said the key ingredient in her recipe for success was the right people—people who were interested in making a difference. Elsie asked Kelly to manage the shop, once Kelly completed her degree in hotel and restaurant management. It would be the stepping-stone prior to her managing a restaurant in New York City, which was her dream. Elsie looked forward to having Kelly manage CLC. It would offer time for her and Chuck to enjoy a few road trips. Yep, life is for the living.

Acknowledgements

Many thanks to Jenna Roe, talented daughter and mind reader, who designed the cover, and my husband, Dave, for your constant support, opinions, and editing. The rest of my family members who may not know it, but provide me with inspiration and encouragement. Sue Lardahl, dear friend, for taking time to read the story in manuscript form prior to the professional editing. And also supplying me with pans of pumpkin bars which provided motivation. Ellie Maas Davis, editor with Pressque, LLC, who encouraged me to expand upon and think beyond. She was an inspirational coach in this venture.

www.ingramcontent.com/pod-product-compliance
Lightning Source LLC
Chambersburg PA
CBHW071543100726
47908CB00004B/1495